A CRIME IN RHYME
and other mysterious fragments

SIMON BRETT

frith
fH
HOUSE

This book was first published in April 2000 by
Frith House Limited

Frith House Limited
Frith House
Burpham
West Sussex
BN18 9RR

ISBN 0-9538410-0-6

©Simon Brett, 2000

The Author asserts his moral right to be
identified as the Author of the Work.

All rights reserved. No part of this book may be
reproduced by any means, electronic or
mechanical, including photocopy or any
information storage and retrieval system without
permission in writing from the publisher.

Designed by Alwyn Thompson-Dyke

Printed by RPM Chichester

CONTENTS

INTRODUCTION 1

A CRIME IN RHYME 4

FRAGMENTS FROM WASTEPAPER BASKETS 49

    Agatha Christie 51

    Raymond Chandler 53

    Charles Dickens 56

WHYDIDNTTHEYDUNNIT 61

    T.S.Eliot 62

    Thomas Hood 66

    Jane Austen 71

    Dylan Thomas 76

To Lucy,
without whom it wouldn't have happened…
…again

INTRODUCTION

I like crime fiction, and I like the traditions of the mystery. Some contemporary writers are a bit sniffy about their antecedents – Agatha Christie, Dorothy L. Sayers, Margery Allingham, the ones who in the Twenties and Thirties defined and refined the genre, with all its anomalies, inconsistencies, snobbishness and political incorrectness. I think they were great. I would not aspire to write like them – nobody nowadays would aspire to write like them – but I respect what they did in shaping the crime novel, and I have a great nostalgic affection for their works.

It is that affection which inspired all the pieces in this short collection. That – and a feeling which can sometimes get lost in contemporary crime literature – that mystery fiction can be fun. Nothing in this book should be taken too seriously. What it offers is a series of variations on fictional crime – answering not so much the question "whodunnit" as the question "whatif…?"

A crime in rhyme

The first - and longest – item in the collection, A Crime In Rhyme, is an idea which I had been nurturing for some time. I'd done lots of speaking engagements in libraries, in bookshops and at mystery conventions, and, although all of them had been well received, I'd often wondered whether there was a presentation other than the straight "author talk" that might be suitable for such events. What if, I thought, I were to write myself a one-man Golden Age whodunnit? How would that go down?

I toyed with the idea for a while, but did nothing. Then, while redecorating my study, I had a bit of time on my hands. Not time for a sustained creative effort like a crime novel, but time for a less linear, more casual and fragmented literary project. Maybe this was the moment to have a go at writing my one-man mystery?

About a week before I started it, worried about my increasing inability to learn lines, I decided to write it in verse. (When I did a lot of amateur dramatics, I used to be very good at memorising whole plays, but it's one of those skills which dissipates with age and without regular practice. If you don't use it, you lose it.) My reasoning was that the predictability of rhyme would make the text stick more readily to the Teflon interior of my brain. (This hope proved unfounded. I have never yet performed A Crime In Rhyme without a copy of the text on a music stand in front of me.)

To motivate myself – or, more accurately, blackmail myself - into doing the actual writing, I booked the show into a venue in a local hotel to perform three lunchtime performances during that year's Arundel Festival. That event was a safe five months away, so round the February and March of 1998 I wrote A Crime In Rhyme and then completely forgot about it.

Only in the July did I remind myself that I had undertaken to perform the show at the end of August, and I wheeled out the script to have a look at it. I read the lines through with mounting horror. It wasn't that I disliked what I'd written; it was the thought of performing it that terrified me.

It's easy enough to write a piece for eleven characters, but what a writer forgets is that performers occasionally want to breathe. I hadn't left any space in the action for that simple necessity.

Still, I persevered, rehearsed away in the privacy of my study, glad that nobody could see me. (Any casual observer would have thought I had gone completely bonkers.) And A Crime In Rhyme had its first public performance at 1.00 pm on Wednesday 26 August 1998 in the Ballroom of the Norfolk Arms Hotel, Arundel, West Sussex. Where it did, I have to say, go extraordinarily well.

Since that time I have performed the show in venues as far apart as Shropshire, Anglesey, New York, Washington and the Greek island of Skyros.

So far it's always been enthusiastically received. Which is why I have taken the step of putting A Crime In Rhyme into book form, and you'll find it here printed along with the programme that is usually presented to its audiences (on the assumption that at least some of them enjoy anagrams).

BRISTOMENT PRODUCTIONS,
in association with SIR BEN MOTT
and BORIS M. NETT
PRESENT

A CRIME IN RHYME
by SIMON BRETT

Lord Raneleigh De Vere, an amateur sleuth	Osbert Mint
Alfie Transom, his chauffeur	Tom St. Brien
Detective Sergeant Yeoman, a local policeman	Ron M. Bettis
Henry, the Duke of Nectingham	Tim Nosbert
Lady Polly Westingham, his fiancée	Toni B. Merts
Count Volensky, an international financier	Ernst Tobim
Lady Olga Trout, the Dowager Duchess's sister	Brit Montes
Hubert Scrivener, the family solicitor	Bert Timson
Colonel Crutchleigh-Prideaux, retired	R.S.M. Bettion
Hopper, the butler	Rob Mittens
Scrappings, the cook	Betti Morns

Director	Tibor Sment
Designer	Brin Osmett
Lighting	T. Brimstone
Music	"T-Bone" Strim
Wardrobe	Teri B. Monts
Stage Manager	Storm Benit
Wardrobe Care	Mrs. Bonetit
Set Construction	O.N.T. Timbers
Production Accountants	Brent, Moist &Co.
Public Relations	Metrobints Ltd.
Marquee	Morbi Tents
Location Catering	Mint Sorbet Caterers
Mr Brett's Hair by	Monti Brest of Mitborne St.

A CRIME IN RHYME

Simon
As an enthusiastic reader of crime fiction, I have frequently been struck that, though there have been whodunnits written in every kind of setting, and in every kind of style, there have been very few, so far as I can tell, perpetrated in verse. Now I'm sure that most people in the world would be happy to let that situation continue.
There'd be no point in changing it,
                                        unless some urge within you
Demanded that a rhyming crime was a matter of priority.
Most people haven't got that urge. Well, I'm in the minority.
But where, you ask, is all this leading?
I'm going to do a dramatised reading.
So please sit back while I rehearse
A whole whodunnit set in verse.
Now, for three-quarters of an hour
You'll hear "The Crime at Cranville Tower",
A tale of foul play and fatality

A crime in rhyme

In a world of cosy unreality.
To a country house our focus draws
In a peaceful England between the Wars.
Picture a pile of palladian splendours,
Full of a mix of rich weekenders,
Each of whom, from first to last,
Has a guilty secret in their past.
Picture a lib'ry of niches and nooks,
And the leather spines of unopened books.
Picture a room that has all that it should -
Tables and lecterns in well-polished wood,
Leather armchairs, in which to lie and snore -
And a well-stabbed Dowager Duchess lying on the floor.
Yes, it's the Dowager Duchess of Nectingham.
(There'll be some rhymes coming –
                            I'm sure you're expecting 'em.)
Picture now a butler, of demeanour haughty and Roman,
Talking to a Policeman - Detective Sergeant Yeoman.

Hopper
Yes, I'm the butler, Sergeant. Go by the name of Hopper.

Detective Sergeant Yeoman
And do you have a first name?

Hopper
                    No, sir.

Detective Sergeant Yeoman
                            Very right and proper.
So tell me quickly what occurred.

Hopper
                            All right, it won't take long.
I came to ask her Grace if I could strike the dinner gong.
I'd had the word from Scrappings –
                She's the cook, I think you've met her.

Detective Sergeant Yeoman
Yes, yes, indeed. And once you've met,
                              'snot easy to forget her.
She's the ugliest woman in the universe.
Is her cooking as bad as her looks?

Hopper
                              No, sir, it's rather worse.

Detective Sergeant Yeoman
Oh dear, oh dear. Well, anyway, you said
You come into the library...

Hopper
                    And found the Duchess dead,
Stabbed, just as you saw her.

Detective Sergeant Yeoman
              And she was on her own?

Hopper
Yes, sir.

Detective Sergeant Yeoman
     So she was killed by "one as yet unknown".

Hopper
Perhaps. If you'll excuse me... Below stairs things are serious.
The murder has provoked all manner of hysterias
Among the housemaids. I must do - as always in these cases -
The proper thing.

Detective Sergeant Yeoman
              And what is that?

A crime in rhyme

Hopper *(going off)*
                        Why, slap the bitches' faces!

Detective Sergeant Yeoman *(waving to him)*
Oh, righty-ho! Now I must check
                     what's what in this here case.
The Dowager Duchess died, a look of horror on her face...
(Trying to remember) And there's one other detail
                            of which I made a note...
Oh yes! A jewelled dagger was sticking in her throat.
Not rushing to conclusions, I think it's safe to say -
Indeed I'll tell the Press : "The Police suspect Foul Play."
But beyond that... Well, I don't know.
                                'Cause for the likes of me
This kind of case is difficult. What I would like to see
Is someone with more intellect to come and help me here...

Lord Raneleigh De Vere
So may I introduce myself - Lord Raneleigh De Vere.

Detective Sergeant Yeoman
Good heavens! Lord Raneleigh? Now come on, tell the truth.
You're not De Vere of world renown,
                          the famous amateur sleuth?

Lord Raneleigh De Vere
I've solved a few odd cases. Yes, I can't deny it's true.

Detective Sergeant Yeoman
So tell me then, Lord Raneleigh, what kind of man are you?

Lord Raneleigh De Vere
I'm honourable, admirable, a polymath - and handsome -
I'm rarely to be seen without
                       my chauffeur sidekick, Transom.

So you recognise my voice,
                    and thus can keep up with the action,
I have a silly accent... of a kind of French extraction.
And when I trap my villains, I am just, but never lenient,
And I'm staying here for this weekend.

Detective Sergeant Yeoman
                    My goodness, that's convenient.

Lord Raneleigh De Vere
And here is Transom, right on cue,
                    my ever faithful henchman.

Detective Sergeant Yeoman
I'm Sergeant Yeoman.

Alfie Transom
            How'd'you do? Come, give my hand a clench, man.
Yes, I'm Alfie Transom, with cauliflower ears,
And a nose like a beacon and knock-knees.
But everyone likes me and buys me beers,
'Cause I'm one of your lovable Cockneys.

Detective Sergeant Yeoman
I'm glad to hear it.

Lord Raneleigh De Vere
            Now let's see.
I really think it's time
That we should end this pleasantry
And examine the scene of the crime.
That is, Sergeant Yeoman, if you don't mind...

Detective Sergeant Yeoman
Mind? Why'd I mind?

A crime in rhyme

Lord Raneleigh De Vere
                  Some policemen, I find,
Have a brain of such narrow diameter,
That professional pride in a homicide
Turns them anti- the talented amateur.
They see my input as intrusion.
Some even have been known
To labour under the delusion
They'd do better on their own.

Detective Sergeant Yeoman
Not me. I know when I'm behind,
And will gladly yield to a mastermind.

Lord Raneleigh De Vere
Stout fellow! What a brick you are!
So tell me what you've got so far.

Detective Sergeant Yeoman
Well, 'twas wicked and highly irregular,
But, after due thought... for these facts I would plump...
That this dagger here severed her jugular,
And come out through her Dowager's hump.
So... into this lib'ry the killer did come,
With a dagger what he had snaffled...
And then... er, um... er, um... er, um...
Apart from that, I'm baffled.

Lord Raneleigh De Vere
Good, excellent! You know your place.

Detective Sergeant Yeoman
What?

Lord Raneleigh De Vere
        Why, Sergeant Yeoman, my friend

To be baffled is all you need do in the case...
Oh, and make an arrest at the end.

Detective Sergeant Yeoman
Well, thanks, my lord. If you don't mind,
                                  I'm off for a cup of tea.

Lord Raneleigh De Vere
How sensible. *(Waving)* No, off you go –
                             and leave the case to me.
Right, Alf, you know what now ensues,
We search this library for clues.

Alfie Transom
Well, all right, guv'nor. Though finding what we seek
In a place like this'll take at least a week,
Until we get that vital clue what helps us to progress.

Lord Raneleigh De Vere
Ah-hah!

Alfie Transom
       Have you found something?

Lord Raneleigh De Vere
                           Yes, I think so, yes.
You see - a shred of winceyette from a gentleman's pyjama,
Expensive fabric made up from the wools of yak and llama,
Inwoven with the whiskers of a Uruguayan Jaguar,
By peasants from a village in the North of Nicaragua.
Yes... The other thing distinctive about this kind of fibre
Is that it's bleached by being immersed
                             in mud from River Tiber,
Then coloured with the marrow of an alligator's tibia.
And the only place to buy it is a little shop in Libya,

A crime in rhyme

That's owned by Hassan in the slums of Tobruk.
But that's all I can tell from a cursory look.

Alfie Transom
My Lord, cor blimey! I'm taken aback!
How'd you know all that?

Lord Raneleigh De Vere
                        Oh, it's just a knack.
(Sniffing the shred)
Good Lord, on this shred there's a slight whiff of Cologne, a-
Nother lead to the pyjamas' owner.
We need more clues, though, Transom.
                        Mustn't stop collecting 'em.
But who comes here?

Alfie Transom
        It is, My Lord, the current Duke of Nectingham.

Lord Raneleigh De Vere
And on his arm, in silks and pearls,
                        so elegantly dressed in 'em?

Alfie Transom
That would be his fiancée, sir, the Lady Polly Westingham.

The Duke of Nectingham
Are you De Vere, the famous sleuth?

Lord Raneleigh De Vere
                        Yes, your Grace, I am.

The Duke of Nectingham
That's frightfully handy. As you see, we're rather in a jam.
In matters of detection I'm afraid I'm just a dummy.

Lord Raneleigh De Vere
Don't worry. I am here.

The Duke of Nectingham
                      Then find who murdered Mummy.

Polly Westingham
Yes, if you could. We'd be so pleased.
                                    It would be frightf'ly jolly.

The Duke of Nectingham
Sorry. Should have introduced you. My fiancée, Polly.

Lord Raneleigh De Vere
Delighted, I am sure.

Polly Westingham
            Me too.

The Duke of Nectingham
                    In matters intellectual,
I must admit that you will find me useless, ineffectual.
My I.Q.'s in single figures, but that causes no distress.
In the British aristocracy, it couldn't matter less.
I'm stupid, but I'm honest, and I've never acted spitefully.

Polly Westingham
But you are awfully sweet.

The Duke of Nectingham
                    Oh, d'you think so, Polly?

Polly Westingham
                                        Frightfully.
It matters not a whit to me that you're so deeply thick.

A crime in rhyme

The Duke of Nectingham
Dear Poll, you say the nicest things.
                                  Oh, crikey, you're a brick.

Lord Raneleigh De Vere *(aside)*
He seems an honest chap - but is to seem enough?
Perhaps he's perpetrating an elaborate double bluff,
And perhaps his air of dumbness
                            is some kind of cunning plot.

The Duke of Nectingham *(to Polly)*
I love you, Bunny Rabbit.

Lord Raneleigh De Vere *(aside)*
                        Then again, perhaps it's not.
But what about the fiancée?
                  (aloud) Excuse me, Lady Westingham.
Do you have family monies?

Polly Westingham
                          Yes, my brokers are investing 'em.

Lord Raneleigh De Vere
And where'd you meet the Duke? Was it somewhere nice?

Polly Westingham
We met at a weekend party at another country hice.

Lord Raneleigh De Vere
And was it love at first sight?
                          Did your hearts at once enmesh?

Polly Westingham
Oh, absolutely! Yes, indeed! It happened in a flesh!
Have you more questions, Lord De Vere?

Lord Raneleigh De Vere
                                        Just one more will suffice.
D'you love the Duke?

Polly Westingham
         Of course. I've said. He's going to be my spice.
Now may we go?

Lord Raneleigh De Vere
         Why, yes, of course. Perhaps more questions later.

The Duke of Nectingham *(going off)*
Yes, anything that helps to find the cad who murdered mater.

Lord Raneleigh De Vere
What say you, Transom? Love's young dream?

Alfie Transom
                   That's certainly the way they seem,
My lord, there's someone coming.

Lord Raneleigh De Vere
                           Yes, a gent in furry tweed
With an outcrop of moustaches that look like tumbleweed.
He seems a trifle angry. Well, his face is rather puce,
And he's about to speak, I think.

Colonel Crutchleigh-Prideaux
                        Goddammit! What the deuce!
According to that slimy creep, the Cranville butler, Hopper,
I hear the Dowager Duchess has somehow come a cropper!

Lord Raneleigh De Vere
That's true. She's dead.

A crime in rhyme

Colonel Crutchleigh-Prideaux
                      Good heavens! How distressin'!

Lord Raneleigh De Vere
Excuse me, sir, but who...
                      do I have the honour of addressin'?

Colonel Crutchleigh-Prideaux
Me name is Crutchleigh-Prideaux. May I present me card?
Colonel in the Coldstreams. Well, I was - now I'm retaard.

Lord Raneleigh De Vere
Very pleased to meet you. I'm Lord Raneleigh De Vere.

Colonel Crutchleigh-Prideaux
 You the detective chappie?

Lord Raneleigh De Vere
                      Yes.

Colonel Crutchleigh-Prideaux
                      I'm very glad you're here.

Lord Raneleigh De Vere
And may I ask why you are?

Colonel Crutchleigh-Prideaux
                    Invited. Furthermore,
Friend of the late Duke. Served with him in the War.

Lord Raneleigh De Vere
And tell me, Colonel Crutchleigh-Prideaux...
Any thoughts who might have killed his widow?

Colonel Crutchleigh-Prideaux
Simple rule I find in all these criminal affairs -

The murderer's a foreigner - or someone below stairs.
So interview the servants - the butler   and the cook...
Or if there's someone foreign here...
>>>>well, that'll be your crook.

Lord Raneleigh De Vere
Thank you, Colonel, that's most helpful.

Colonel Crutchleigh-Prideaux
>>>>Ssh! I hear a sound.

Alfie Transom
A man's come into the library. Ah-hah, he's looking round.

Lord Raneleigh De Vere
Why's he entered? What's he up to? What is his intent?

Alfie Transom
He's up to mischief, that's for sure.
>>>>He's a foreign-looking gent.

Colonel Crutchleigh-Prideaux
Your murderer!

Lord Raneleigh De Vere
>>>>Excuse me, sir. What are you doing here?

Count Volensky
How honoured I am to meet you, Lord Raneleigh De Vere.

Lord Raneleigh De Vere
You know my name.

Count Volensky
>>>>Why, so I do. Your fame has spread abroad -
Your solving of the Prinknash Case is something I applaud.

A crime in rhyme

How cunningly you recognised that almond cyanide smell
Was in the Bakewell Tart.

Lord Raneleigh De Vere
      'Twas nothing. Who are you, though, tell?

Count Volensky
My name is Count Volensky - with a "v" and not a "w",
And I was born in... somewhere.
      No, the details need not trouble you.

Lord Raneleigh De Vere
And how d'you spend your time?

Colonel Crutchleigh-Prideaux *(sniffing)*
      I'm smelling something funny.

Count Volensky
Oh, I do this and that. It is all concerned with money.
Yes, I handle lots of money - clients' money - and my own.

Colonel Crutchleigh-Prideaux
My God, the bounder's simply reeking of Cologne!

Lord Raneleigh De Vere
And you're staying for the weekend?

Count Volensky
      Yes, indeed. It was my plan
To take part in those pastimes which befit a gentleman.

Colonel Crutchleigh-Prideaux
He's no gentleman!

Count Volensky
   And now excuse me... I hope you will not mi-ond.

I'm going to read 'The Times' - if it's been properlily ironed.

Lord Raneleigh De Vere
Goodbye!

Colonel Crutchleigh-Prideaux
    Ha, ha, ha, ha!

Lord Raneleigh De Vere
        Sorry, Colonel, what's the joke?

Colonel Crutchleigh-Prideaux
Well, this one's easy for you, ain't it?

Lord Raneleigh De Vere
        Sorry?

Colonel Crutchleigh-Prideaux
            He's your bloke.
He did it. Case is closed - all nice and simple for the coroner.

Lord Raneleigh De Vere
But why?

Colonel Crutchleigh-Prideaux
    For heaven's sake! Because he's Johnnie Foreigner
He must have done it. Oh, come on, it isn't very tricky.

Lord Raneleigh De Vere
But have you any evidence?

Colonel Crutchleigh-Prideaux
        Now you're just being picky.
Listen! He's not British - and did you smell that odour?
He wears Cologne. He did it.
        'Bye – I need a Scotch and soda.

Alfie Transom
D'you 'ear that, guv? What racism!
                                        What narrow, blinkered views!
That's the kind of bigotry that no one can excuse!
The Colonel's accusations are just prejudice and spite!
Don't you agree, my Lord?

Lord Raneleigh De Vere
                          Oh yes... Of course, he could be right.
I've seen some of the houseguests. There must be others still.

Alfie Transom
I'm sure they'll all be present for the Reading of the Will.

Simon
And so they were. With one or two
                            whom we have yet to meet -
There's Scrappings - she's the cook,
                            who's left the kitchen's heat -
With something noxious simmering in her Aga -
To talk to Lady Olga Trout, who's really almost gaga.

Lady Olga Trout
Tell me, Scrappings, where's my sister? Is she on a cruise?

Scrappings
She dead, my lady.

Lady Olga Trout
           Really? Well, that is terrific news.
From the moment I was born, I never liked Matilda,
And, if I ever got the chance, you know,
                                I would have killed 'er.
He, he, he, he!

Hubert Scrivener
    Huc-hm, huc-hm. Now your attention, please.

Lady Olga Trout
Who's that in the black suit that's gone
        all baggy at the knees?

Scrappings
It's Hubert Scrivener.

Lady Olga Trout
    Who's he? Another bally visitor?

Scrappings
No, no, my lady, he's the Duchess's solicitor.

Hubert Scrivener
Are we ready? Can we start? Your Grace, are you all set?

The Duke of Nectingham
Am I, Polly?

Polly Westingham
  Yes, you are.

Hubert Scrivener
    So I may start?

The Duke of Nectingham
       You bet!

Hubert Scrivener
You are all here, I see, both friends and kith and kin.
Are you sitting comfortably? Then I will begin.
This is the last will and testament
Of Matilda, Duchess of Nectingham.
Its provisions will not, as I estimate,

Surprise you - there's sense and respect in 'em.
"To my son in his ducal vestiment,
Wife and heirs - if alive or expecting'em,
I leave all my estate as bequest. (I meant
Not to be charged with neglecting 'em).
To Hopper my butler and Scrappings my cook,
Each gets five hundred pounds, rather less than they took
From my purse while alive. But as God my judge is,
This is no time to harbour grudges.
And to Colonel Crutchleigh-Prideaux, also known as 'Bill',
Whose company I always found infernal,
But who was very keen to be remembered in my will,
I say, 'Yes, I remember you.
      And that's it. Bad luck, Colonel.'"

Colonel Crutchleigh-Prideaux
That's scandalous! It's libellous!
      The will's terms must be changed!
At the time the Duchess wrote it,
      she was obviously deranged.

Hubert Scrivener
No, Colonel, she was of sound mind.
      But I should make it clear
'Twas on a legal matter that she had called me here.
The Duchess wished to change her will.
      But death has now prevented
The alterations she proposed from being implemented.

Lord Raneleigh De Vere
What changes did she wish to make?
      Where would the money go?

Hubert Scrivener
That's something now, Lord Raneleigh,
      that we can never know.

Simon
A scene of consternation then ensued,
                              as you might guess,
With all the suspects shouting in confusion and distress,
And in the chaos no one saw De Vere had withdrawn
To discuss the case with Transom on the Cranville croquet lawn.

Lord Raneleigh De Vere *(after the Tonk of a croquet ball being hit)*
It's your go, Transom.

Alfie Transom
              Fanking you, my Lord.

Lord Raneleigh De Vere
You know, I think our Russian Count's a fraud...

Alfie Transom
What, old Volensky? Frough the 'oop - *(Tonk)* - damn!

Lord Raneleigh De Vere
Yes. I have just received a cablegram,
From Moscow, where I focused my enquiries,
And Jasper Henry Pilkington Esquire is
Our so-called Count - or that is my belief.

Alfie Transom
And what's he do?

Lord Raneleigh De Vere
              He is a jewel thief.
(Tonk - tonk-tonk-tonk-tonk) Ah, that went through.
Righty-ho, Transom, over to you.

A crime in rhyme

Alfie Transom
Fanks, my Lord. Now if I just prod it,
I should be fine. *(Pause, Tonk)* Sod it!

Lord Raneleigh De Vere
I had a word with Hopper, when I took him to one side,
About Volensky's movements on the day the Duchess died.
The Count was very poorly - or that is what he said.
He stayed in his pyjamas and he spent the day in bed.

Alfie Transom
Pyjamas? How much would I bet
                They match that shred of winceyette?

Lord Raneleigh De Vere
They do. So... Pilkington came down the stairs to steal.
The Duchess then surprised him. To conceal
His crime, he struck her dead,
And hurried back off to his bed.

Alfie Transom
It's great! It works! My Lord, you're just the best!
But tell me, why d'you look so dismal and depressed?

Lord Raneleigh De Vere
It's simply this, my friend. It sounds a trifle trite,
But I'd hate to admit that the Colonel might be right.
Still, never mind. I'll try to look more merry,
And beard the Count over pre-prandial sherry.

Alfie Transom
Yeah, that's the way. Just as the glasses clink,
You'll get him.

Lord Raneleigh De Vere
           Yes. *(Pause - Tonk, tonk)* My game, I think.

Simon
So again the suspects gather - now in long dress or DJ -
While Hopper passes sherry on a Georgian silver tray.

Count Volensky
How interesting. This cut-glass chalice
Comes from the late Tsar's Winter Palace.
In Britain, stealing foreign glass is
A hobby of the upper classes.

Colonel Crutchleigh-Prideaux
Now, listen, one of my aversions
Is foreigners casting aspersions!

Count Volensky
You listen!

The Duke of Nectingham
      Please! Now let's please be pleasant.
We want no rows with ladies present.

Count Volensky
Ladies? Where are they? Please show me.

Lady Olga Trout
I'm a lady. Don't you know me?

Count Volensky
You have titles. I'm not contesting 'em,
But the same's not true of... Polly Westingham.
Lady Polly? Is that what you suppose?

The Duke of Nectingham
Sir, are you looking for a bloody nose?

A crime in rhyme

Count Volensky
I've met this girl before. Don't be fooled by her hypocrisy.
Her birth was very far from the British aristocracy.

Lord Raneleigh De Vere
So where was it you met her?

Count Volensky
                      I'll tell you where I fount 'er,
Working hard at Harrods - on the handbag counter.

Lady Olga Trout
A hand-baaag?

The Duke of Nectingham
        Why, you blighter! You're just asking to be beaten!

Count Volensky
Try, Duke. You will regret it...
                      'cause I learned to box at Eton.
Come, Duke, put up your dukes!

The Duke of Nectingham
                     All right. I'm now so mad
I'll smash your bally head in, you dirty rotten cad!

Polly Westingham
No, hold it there!

The Duke of Nectingham
        Don't worry, love. I'm younger, faster, stronger.

Polly Westingham
No, no, I cannot let this lying go on longer.
I'll tell the truth - and face the worst.
                            It's always true that right'll

Triumph in the end. I haven't got a title.

All
(GASP)

Polly Westingham
Of noble blood within my veins, there's not a single particle.

Lady Olga Trout
You know, I never thought she was the genuine article.

Polly Westingham
I was not born with a silver spoon in my mouth.
A mouth, in fact, where I was born,
                                was called a 'north and south'.
The only spoon that I possessed was
                                one that you'd put porridge in
Yes, I am just a shopgirl, and of very humble origin -
And what you see before you is all I've to my name.

The Duke of Nectingham *(Taken aback)*
Oh. *(After a pause)* Well, never mind, old Polly.
                                    I love you just the same.

Polly Westingham
Oh... Henry!

The Duke of Nectingham
        Polly!

Alfie Transom
This is jolly.

Lord Raneleigh De Vere
Yes, it's all exceedingly charming,
                               and I'd hate to break the spell,

A crime in rhyme

But, Count, you knew she was a shopgirl.
                            Did the Duchess know as well?

Count Volensky
I told her, yes.

Lord Raneleigh De Vere
           Which news might merit
A change of will, so she'd disinherit
Her son, if he remained persistent
In his plans to marry a shop assistant.

Count Volensky
Perhaps.

Lord Raneleigh De Vere
    So why'd you tell her?

Count Volensky
                    Malice.
And now a sip from this golden chalice...

Lord Raneleigh De Vere
Before you sip, I'd like to ascertain
A couple of points perhaps you could explain -
A) Why you've come here in disguise,
And B) Why, the day the Duchess dies,
You creep down to the library when you're in theory ill.
Perhaps you can explain that...?

Count Volensky
                    Most certainly I will.
Lying on my sickbed, with a nasty dose of 'flu,
I hear a scream from downstairs. I go down.
                          Well, wouldn't you?
So, following the sound, I push the lib'ry door

And then - I see the Duchess lying on the floor.
I stood in shock. I stood amazed. My heartbeat missed a blip.
And then - excuse me while I have a little sip...
(He drinks.)
Then - as I stand there frozen - I hear a sudden noise and -
Ergh... ergh... ergh-ergh-erg-ergh...
        Goddammit, I've been poisoned!
(He dies.)

All
(GASP)

Lord Raneleigh De Vere
All right, all right. Now, no one move!
We'll need some evidence to prove
Who murdered this notorious conman, thief and fraud.
Transom, collect the glasses.

Alfie Transom
        Certainly, my lord.
I've one - and two - and three - four - five - and then six -

Lord Raneleigh De Vere
Good. Excellent. Now take them to forensics.

Alfie Transom
Yes, sir.

Colonel Crutchleigh-Prideaux
  De Vere, now that Volensky's dead, the case is done.
        He must've killed Matilda.

Lord Raneleigh De Vere
He didn't.

A crime in rhyme

Colonel Crutchleigh-Prideaux
    What? Then do you know who killed 'er?

Lord Raneleigh De Vere
Not quite.

Colonel Crutchleigh-Prideaux
    But he's the only dago in the frame,
If not him, then a servant - their behaviour's much the same.

Lord Raneleigh De Vere
Oh, by the way, the Count - so-called –
                                was not a Count at all.

Colonel Crutchleigh-Prideaux
Well, that's your Johnnie Foreigner.
                            Surprised he had the gall.

Lord Raneleigh De Vere
What's more, he wasn't Russian.

Colonel Crutchleigh-Prideaux
                        Was he Chinky then, or Jap?

Lord Raneleigh De Vere
No, British.

Colonel Crutchleigh-Prideaux
    Didn't I always say he was a splendid chap?

Lord Raneleigh De Vere
Ladies and gentlemen, your attention, please.
Now Count Volensky's dead, if everyone agrees,
I'll need, in order to complete investigation,
To question each of you for information.
Meanwhile, forget this crime you've just observed.

Right, Hopper.

Hopper
     Yes, my Lord. *(He bangs a gong.)* Dinner is served.

Simon
The houseguests then, assembled saints and sinners,
Sit down to another of Scrappings' dreadful dinners.
Some tense as a spring, some cool as a cucumber,
Knowing that there's a murderer in their number.
And Lord De Vere, whose lazy glances flick
Beneath his hooded eyelids, doesn't miss a trick,
Until he's told that D.S. Yeoman's brought
The interim forensic lab report.

Lord Raneleigh De Vere
They've checked the fatal vessel
                         from which Volensky swallowed?

Detective Sergeant Yeoman
Oh, yes, my Lord, and all correct procedures
                             have been followed.
They tested it forensic'ly by chemical analysis
With the very latest methods on which they place reliance.

Lord Raneleigh De Vere
And they've identified it?

Detective Sergeant Yeoman
                      Yes. We know what's in the chalice is
Most certainly a poison that's unknown to medical science.

Lord Raneleigh De Vere
It all comes clear!

A crime in rhyme

Detective Sergeant Yeoman
    Oh, does it?

Lord Raneleigh De Vere
              Yes, as clear as clear can be!

Detective Sergeant Yeoman
I'll take your word for that, my Lord.
              It's still not clear to me.

Lord Raneleigh De Vere
Ha, ha, ha, ha! The game's afoot! I must be on my way!

Detective Sergeant Yeoman
Goodbye! But, given this moment alone,
        there's something that I'd like to say.
Life down my station's simple.
        What don't come through the door is
The kind of folks you read about in them detective stories.
I've never met a hitman, or a terrorist guerrilla,
A drug-dealer, a cannibal, or even a serial killer.
What we get more of down here is honey stole from bees,
And knickers nicked off washing lines,
        and cats got stuck up trees.
I've never even seen a bounty hunter or plea-bargainer.
I don't write poems... and what is more...
        I've never listened to Wagener.
Evening, 'all. Cheerio.

Simon
And now we see the supersleuth De Vere
Move very quickly, as the dénouement draws near.
He questions first, as they enjoy their sport,
The Duke and Polly on the tennis court.

Lord Raneleigh De Vere
Tell me, your Grace. *(Plomp)* Oh, super shot!
D'you know what jewels your mother'd got?

The Duke of Nectingham *(running around)*
They stayed in vaults - *(Plomp)* - in the banks.

Lord Raneleigh De Vere
Oh, what a smashing forehand!

The Duke of Nectingham
                        Thanks.

Lord Raneleigh De Vere
And, Polly, could you spare a mo?

Polly Westingham
Of course. *(Plomp)*

The Duke of Nectingham *(distant)*
            That's out!

Polly Westingham
                   Oh, bother! Blow!
Second serve! *(Plomp)* Ooh, an ace!

Lord Raneleigh De Vere
Just one question on the case...

Polly Westingham
Yes, ask away. *(Plomp)* Good one!

The Duke of Nectingham *(distant)*
                      Rather!

A crime in rhyme

Lord Raneleigh De Vere
Did you ever meet your father?

Polly Westingham
No. But every birthday, since first I put my bib on,
He'd send a birthday present, wrapped in thin pink ribbon.

Lord Raneleigh De Vere
What kind of present?

Polly Westingham
              Clothes... a scarf... a glove...

Lord Raneleigh De Vere
Thank you, My Lady.

Polly Westingham
              (*Plomp*) My game! Six-love!

Lord Raneleigh De Vere
So... next I'll beard the shifty butler, Hopper.
Now tell me, man. You are a famed eavesdropper.

Hopper
Perhaps.

Lord Raneleigh De Vere
      The Duchess... did she blow her top
To hear that Polly once worked in a shop?

Hopper
She wasn't pleased. She made a furious scene.
It made her think of what she once had been.

Lord Raneleigh De Vere
What's that?

Hopper
                Her Grace, before her marriage
Worked in a hairdresser's in Harwich.

Lord Raneleigh De Vere
Ah-hah! Beneath her noble trappings,
She was a pleb. I'll speak to Scrappings.
Tell me, Scrappings, given your cuisine
Is of the ghastliest there's ever been,
Did you cheat to keep your job?

Scrappings
                    There was no need of cheating.
The British upper classes never notice what they're eating.

Lord Raneleigh De Vere
Ah-hah! That's true. The truth will always out.
Now I must speak to Lady Olga Trout.
Lady Olga Trout, you didn't like your sister?

Lady Olga Trout
Matilda was a pain, a proper little blister.

Lord Raneleigh De Vere
But did she in her life perform one kindly act, perhaps?

Lady Olga Trout
No. Well, yes, she kept on Scrappings
                    after Scrappings' little lapse.

Lord Raneleigh De Vere
Ah-hah! How readily she picked up the clue that I'd given 'er.
And now it's time to have a word with M. Hubert Scrivener.
M. Scrivener, for how long have you
                    been the Cranville Tower lawyer?

A crime in rhyme

Hubert Scrivener
The late Duke's father was my first employer.

Lord Raneleigh De Vere
And what about your sex-life?

Hubert Scrivener
       Huh. You're a rude inquisitor.

Lord Raneleigh De Vere
Your sex-life?

Hubert Scrivener
   I don't have one. After all, I'm a solicitor.

Lord Raneleigh De Vere
Come, what about the ladies? Did you not once inveigle
One up into your bedroom?

Hubert Scrivener
      No, that would be illegal.
You'll get no witness, whatever you suggest. If I
Had touched a woman, she wouldn't dare to testify.
I know the law. No one would admit that I kissed 'em.

Lord Raneleigh De Vere
So that's another triumph for the British legal system.
Ah-hah! It all comes out. Soon nothing will be hid. Oh
Damn, now I must talk to Colonel Crutchleigh-Prideaux.
Colonel, now the Count is dead...

Colonel Crutchleigh-Prideaux
       Good riddance too, say I!

Lord Raneleigh De Vere
 ...d'you have another suspect?

Colonel Crutchleigh-Prideaux
                      Yes, I cannot tell a lie.

Lord Raneleigh De Vere
Then who do you think did it?

Colonel Crutchleigh-Prideaux
                      I will tell you who.
I knew it was a foreigner. The murderer was... you!

Lord Raneleigh De Vere
Ah...hah! Well, thank you, Colonel,
                      for your answer to my query.
It really is a most... a most unusual theory.
I've worked it out! I've worked it out! My brain it is so huge!
I need to share this moment with a deferential stooge!
Transom!

Alfie Transom
      My Lord?

Lord Raneleigh De Vere
                  I've all I need!
Forgive my wild elation.

Alfie Transom
You've cracked the case?

Lord Raneleigh De Vere
                  I have indeed.
No more investigation.
I know the who, the where, the which,
The wherefore and the whether.
I have pulled tight the final stitch.
My case has come together!

A crime in rhyme

Alfie Transom
There was a motive?

Lord Raneleigh De Vere
                Yes. Concealed.

Alfie Transom
Was it blackmail, greed or bribery?

Lord Raneleigh De Vere
Wait, Transom. All will be revealed
When they're summoned to the libr'ry.

Simon
So picture now that final scene...
                The tense, expectant mood
Spares no one from its clutches,
For the houseguests gathered round include
The one who killed the Duchess.
They sit, all stiff and mannerly,
As they listen to Lord Raneleigh.

Lord Raneleigh De Vere
You may be wondering why I've asked you here.

Colonel Crutchleigh-Prideaux
No, I think we probably know, Lord Raneleigh De Vere.

Lord Raneleigh De Vere
All right. In such a case it does not pay to linger.
I know who killed the Duchess, and soon I'll point a finger
At one of you. By processes of logic and deduction,
By sudden strokes of genius and mental reconstruction,
I have the proof to take our murderer to the scaffold.
You with me, Sergeant Yeoman?

Detective Sergeant Yeoman
                           To tell the truth, I'm baffled.

Lord Raneleigh De Vere
Good. The murder was done for the love of Polly.
So she'd have a share of the Cranville lolly,
To keep the will unchanged - it had to end in slaughter
In order to protect - an illegitimate daughter.

All
(GASP)

Lord Raneleigh De Vere
But who's this daughter?
                     What is more, who is the daughter's mother?
Scrappings, I'll find the truth out, one way or the other,
What happened to your baby just as soon as
                                  you had dropped it?

Scrappings
I couldn't stand the shame, so I had the child adopted.

Lord Raneleigh De Vere
I put it to you, Scrappings, that your youthful lapse or folly

Produced that lady over there
                          - the one who's known as Polly.

All
(GASP)

Scrappings
Well, she could be my daughter, her mother could be I,
If there's a little strawberry mark upon her outer thigh.

A crime in rhyme

Lord Raneleigh De Vere
So, is there?

The Duke of Nectingham *(After a pause)*
> Why'd'you look at me? Good Lord, I've no idea.

Lord Raneleigh De Vere
Well, she is your fiancée.

The Duke of Nectingham
> But I haven't seen her rear.
Unmarried chaps don't know what ladies look like, as a rule...
At least, they don't if they have been to
> English public school.

Polly Westingham
But I once saw my body...

The Duke of Nectingham *(Shocked)*
> Polly!

Polly Westingham
> ...when the bathroom door was locked,
There was a mirror in there...

The Duke of Nectingham
> Well, my goodness me, I'm shocked.

Polly Westingham
...and I looked down at my -

The Duke of Nectingham
> There's no need to say the word!

Polly Westingham
...and there I saw -

a crime in rhyme

The Duke of Nectingham
    Don't say it!

Polly Westingham
        Henry, don't be so absurd!
I saw a mark...

The Duke of Nectingham
    Well, that's a shock!

Polly Westingham
       ...a red mark...

The Duke of Nectingham
        That's another!

Polly Westingham
...and it <u>was</u> shaped like a strawberry.

Scrappings
      My little baby!

Polly Westingham
        Mother!

Lord Raneleigh De Vere
A mother found! Find who's the father –
      then my case is built.
A father who cast off his child, but felt sufficient guilt
To send her, on each birthday, a pink-beribboned token.
A father who'd no wish to see his child's engagement broken,
For she had risen through the ranks, from poverty in steerage
To life in First Class, and would soon be
        entering the peerage.
So what the Duchess then proposed,
      our murderer found abhorrent.
And when she said she'd change her will,

A crime in rhyme

                        she'd signed her own death warrant.
But Count Volensky saw the crime, and that's the reason why
it Had to be that he was poisoned, just to keep him quiet.
Then who's this man who hatched this plan, and stabbed with such ferocity?
Who was it? Who? I'll give a clue to tease your curiosity.
Which profession lacks morals and has no beliefs,
And uses pink ribbons to tie up its briefs?
Yes, our murderer, who wanted his bastard to live in a
Mansion like this was, of course - Hubert Scrivener!

Scrappings
Lawks-a-mussy!

Alfie Transom
          Strike a light!

Colonel Crutchleigh-Prideaux
Jove!

The Duke of Nectingham
     Heavens!

Polly Westingham
          Crikey!

Detective Sergeant Yeoman
              Cripes!

Lady Olga Trout
                      He's right!

Hopper
At least the butler didn't do it!

Detective Sergeant Yeoman
How did you know, though?

Lord Raneleigh De Vere
                      Nothing to it.
The butler didn't murder her, because his eyes were brown,
And, as for his bifocals, well, he wore them upside down.
It couldn't be the cook, because her middle name was Nell,
And the blood group of her sister rules out
                                  Olga Trout as well.
The temp'rature I measured in the pepper in the cruet
Meant that neither Polly nor the current Duke could do it.
I'm exonerated by the entry in my journal,
And the price of leeks in Norwich meant it couldn't be
                                  the Colonel!
Besides, it's an acknowledged fact, from
                              Cape Horn to Alaska,
That the Venezuelan fruitbat doesn't spawn in Madagascar!
Ah-hah! Ha-ha!

Detective Sergeant Yeoman
    Good heavens! It's so easy when you hear it simplified.
Why di'n't I work that out?

Lord Raneleigh De Vere
                    Well, let's leave that on one side...
I've named the murderer,
                      safe and sure there'll be no reassessing.
(When it comes to mystery fiction,
                            the death penalty's a blessing!)
So, Hubert Scrivener,
                do you contest my reasoned accusation?

Hubert Scrivener
No, no.

A crime in rhyme

Detective Sergeant Yeoman
    Oh, well. I say, my Lord, Shall I take him to the station?

Lord Raneleigh De Vere
In just a little while. But first, in this adjacent study,
I'll talk to Hubert man to man.

Hubert Scrivener
                      I'm sorry. This is bloody.
A bloody mess.

Lord Raneleigh De Vere
                Yes, I agree. I think I could provide...
A possible solution...

Hubert Scrivener
          What?

Lord Raneleigh De Vere
                I thought of... suicide.

Hubert Scrivener
Oh, would that help to make amends?

Lord Raneleigh De Vere
It'd certainly tie up a few loose ends.
The thing is, death by hanging makes awful lot of mess.
Then the papers... Save your daughter from
                      a great deal of distress.

Hubert Scrivener
So, how to solve my problem...?

Lord Raneleigh De Vere
                I'm a famous problem-solver.

I've a reputation for it. Well, good heavens - a revolver.
That's handy.

Hubert Scrivener
   Handy?

Lord Raneleigh De Vere
      Yes. And loaded - ring-a-ding!
It's perfect for the chap who wants to...
       'do the decent thing.'
(He looks elaborately at his watch.)
Is that the time? Must dress for dinner. Sorry, I must go.

Hubert Scrivener
So, see you later?

Lord Raneleigh De Vere
   No. Don't really think so. No.

Hubert Scrivener
So what to do? Go through the courts –
      might get off on appeal...?
But if I do, this tale will never reach its final reel.
Besides... takes one to know one... I've a certain paranoia
From the knowledge my defence case
      would be handled by a lawyer.
No, no, I know my duty. Better shooting than to hang...
Yes, I'll end, not with a whimper, but with a resounding -
(A gunshot is heard.)

Lord Raneleigh De Vere *(very breezily)*
Transom, I've solved the case, I've filled the idle hour,
And now I'm rather bored with being
      here at Cranville Tower.
What gives?

A crime in rhyme

Alfie Transom
        By chance, my Lord, I've had a cablegram
From the Major-Domo of the Emperor of Siam.
His Chinese mistress has been found dead in her negligée,
With a G-string tight around her neck –
                and the police suspect foul play.
He hardly dares to ask, but if Lord Raneleigh De Vere -

Lord Raneleigh De Vere
We'll need some airline tickets!

Alfie Transom
                My Lord, I've got them here.
There's lots of suspects.

Lord Raneleigh De Vere
        Let's toward 'em!
Anything to stave off boredom!

Simon
So, as De Vere and Transom go to solve another mystery,
The case of Cranville Tower can be consigned to history.
For those who got the murderer right,
                I'll say, before you go,
There are no prizes - save perhaps a priggish inner glow.
Still, after many a moral twist and tortured convolution,
We've ended with a satisfying, ethical solution
(Though if you were to question
        all its details and particulars,
You'd realise its reasoning was totally ridiculous!).
By looking at my watch,
        I see that's all that we've got time for,
But a simple moral outcome
            is what people turn to crime for.
It's the comforting murder mystery

                              of the warm domestic hearth,
The cheering cup of tea, and the long, relaxing bath.
The murder's solved - to make things neat,
                              the murderer's also dead,
And every one of us... can sleep securely in our bed.

FRAGMENTS FROM WASTEPAPER BASKETS

A few years ago I wrote a book whose contents had all been found in the wastepaper baskets of the famous. At least that was the premise. In fact, *The Wastepaper Basket Archive* was just an excuse for me to indulge my taste for parody and other literary jokes.

The book contained such gems as :

King Arthur's attempt to do a seating plan with a Square Table,

A crumpled sheet from Samuel Beckett's wastepaper basket, which read :

"ACT ONE
SCENE ONE
Enter GODOT",

And the following rejected early draft by William Wordsworth :

"I wandered lonely as a cloud
That rains upon the Daddies and the Mums,
When all at once I saw a crowd,
A host of gold chrysanthemums."

A crime in rhyme

Needless to say, given my taste for crime fiction, one or two of the items had a mystery background. The first reprinted here comes from the wastepaper basket of perhaps the best-known of all whodunnit writers.

A CANCELLED DRAFT OF AGATHA CHRISTIE'S WILL

This is the last will and testament of me, Agatha Christie.

I give and bequeath all of my estate, and the royalties for fifty years after my death, to my long-lost nephew Eric, from Australia… unless he dies within a month of my death, in which case the property shall go to his illegitimate brother Henry, the solicitor…

If, however, both brothers die within a month of my death, the beneficiary of this will shall be my housekeeper, Winifred Carston… who is really the daughter of my doctor, Marmaduke Dollington…

In the event of Winifred dying within a month of my death, her father will inherit… but only if he is reconciled with his estranged wife, Daphne…

If, however, Daphne dies before the month is up, the police should be called and, after Marmaduke's arrest, my estate should go to his niece, my long-suffering nurse, Betty…

Should Betty die in suspicious circumstances…

… A crime in rhyme

Part of the fun of *The Wastepaper Basket Archive* was that the reader had to work out why the particular piece had been thrown away. For example, why didn't Raymond Chandler allow the following fragment to get into print?

FROM RAYMOND CHANDLER'S
WASTEPAPER BASKET

"What's your name?" he asked in a voice you could have scoured a soup pan with.

"Marlowe," I said. "Philip Marlowe."

The girl giggled with private merriment. Her lashes caressed her cheeks. She was neatly put together, and had been told so many times. She wore a navy-blue business suit with creases sharp enough to cut salami real thin. Her dark eyes were cold but looked as if they might come to the boil if the right flame was lit under them.

The man's eyes didn't look as if they'd heat up in a blast-furnace. He was about six feet four with none of it wasted in fat or compassion. The grey flannel suit he wore looked like it was having trouble holding him in. I got the feeling it wasn't only suits that'd have that problem.

"O.K., Mr. Marlowe. So what's your business?"

I said nothing. I let out a little cloud of cigarette smoke and watched it melt in the rather dim light of the office.

"I asked you a question," said the man.

I sank my lower jaw down on to my chest. "I'm thinking about an answer."

The girl liked that. She seemed to like seeing her boss cut down to size. I got the feeling doing a lot of that could be the way to bring her dark eyes to the boil. I also got the feeling it could be the way to get dead.

A crime in rhyme

A flash from the man's eyes stopped her giggle before it dared come out.

"Listen, Marlowe. I don't have a lot of time. Don't fool around. Tell me why you're here."

I put one of my cards with the tommy gun in the corner on his desk. He looked at it as if I'd shoved last week's cheese sandwich up his nose.

"So you're a private detective. What's that to me?"

It was time to hit him with the facts. "I've been hired by Darnley Bombeck to find his daughter."

The facts hurt when they hit him. He gave me a look which ought to have made an exit-wound somewhere round the small of my back. He tried to recover himself, but didn't make up nearly enough ground.

"Why you telling me this, Mr. Marlowe?"

I blew a lungful of cigarette smoke at him. Maybe he'd never liked the taste, or if he had he'd gone off it.

I said : "I thought you might be interested."

He stared at me for a second or two. Then he said sharply : "As a private detective, what do you charge?"

"A hundred down as retainer – that's when I'm working with strangers. Then twenty-five a day, plus expenses."

"That include the car?"

"Eight cents a mile."

He nodded, his heavy jaw brushing against his powder-blue tie. "That's not a lot," he said in a thinking kind of voice.

I shrugged. The girl ran her fingers through her hair. She did it as if she'd rather someone else was doing it for her.

"Look, Marlowe," the man said. "I'd pay a lot more than that for you *not* to find Bombeck's daughter." I said nothing. "A thousand dollars?"

He let it hang in the air like bait. I shook my head. "Sorry. You got the wrong man."

"Two thousand dollars?"

"Ah," I said. "*Now* you're talking."

FROM CHARLES DICKENS' WASTEPAPER BASKET

One of the great mysteries of English literature is *The Mystery of Edwin Drood*, the novel on which Charles Dickens was working at the time of his death in 1870. Only twenty-two chapters remained.

Dickens left few clues as to how he proposed to finish the book, and there have been many attempts to second-guess his intentions.

The plot is extremely complicated, but the main question it demands is : "What has happened to Edwin Drood?"

He has disappeared in mysterious circumstances. Murder is suspected, but not proved – no body can be found. Is he alive? Is he dead? Where has he gone?

For over a century these questions have remained unanswered. How fortunate that when I was recently doing some research at Gadshill, where Dickens died, I found an old wastepaper basket and in it a sheaf of manuscript papers, of which what follows is a transcription.

THE MYSTERY OF EDWIN DROOD
CHAPTER 23
The Veiled Lady

London. Summer still choking the city breathless. Summer mixing dust with the smoke spilling down from chimney pots. Summer adding the shimmer of heat-haze to this clogging compound of dust and smoke, stirring a witches' brew of bright opacity, veiling, fragmenting and trembling the vistas of towers and terraces, corner shops and cathedrals, bridges and barges, tobacconists and tenements. Summer breaking the images of the city into slivers of coloured glass, changing the picture with the twist of a wrist, like some giant child's hand, experimenting on Christmas morning with its newly-unwrapped kaleidoscope.

Dust everywhere. Dust making tiny archipelagos on the surface of cold water in bedroom bowls. Dust dulling the shine of tables and cabinets, tall-boys and cake-stands, coffers and closets. Dust in the kitchens, mocking the cooks' mania for cleanliness; dust in the drawing-rooms, caught as slow-moving motes by the diagonals of morning sunlight, biding their time, spinning gently, abstracted, selecting the destinations on which they will descend. Dust in the eyes and ears and throats of the waking world; dust tickling at early morning mouths, calling out the coughs with the peremptory despatch of an usher in a court-room. Dust also summoning up from their cells a dirty company of spits, hawks and hacks.

fragments from wastepaper baskets

And dust stirred by the hem of the dress of the veiled lady who walks the early morning streets from the docks towards a hybrid hotel at the dingy end of Cheesemaker Street. Her veil adds another distortion to the refractions of the dust, and London looms, ominous and lowering, like a land seen in a dream, through the unfamiliar net which curtains her face. Her clothes, too, the heavy swatches of cloth across her shoulders, the long swish of skirts against the ground, all feel strange. She seems a creature from the land of dreams, swimming on the surface of the heat-haze.

That behind the veil the lady is thinking, and that the thoughts of one recently arrived from foreign shores must be vivid, is not to be doubted. But can we know the nature of her thoughts? Do they run on John Jasper? Is Mr. Grewgious allowed access to the private rooms of her mind? Does Mr. Crisparkle loll about there, making himself at home, perhaps sitting down in an armchair, with his slippered feet up on one of the mental tables of that secret place?

Alas, we cannot know; and even if we tried to read the mind's construction in the lady's face, we would be frustrated by the dark curtain of her veil.

If her face is denied to us, her hands may perhaps speak volumes of information. Are they the scarred hands of a serving-woman, the white hands of a lady? Do they bear encrustations of jewellery, are they legitimised by a wedding ring?

Alas, we cannot know; for as her face is shrouded by a veil, so are her hands hidden by gloves of kid.

But let us follow her. Yes, perhaps if we follow her through the dusty doorway of her sad hotel, we may be allowed to share a little of her secret. To the clerk she goes, a moping, fat boy, hardly awake; with almost masculine imperatives, she commands a room. Her travelling baggage will be coming in a fly from the docks; she gives the fat boy instructions for its disposition. Wheezing a little, he leads her up the dusty stairs

A crime in rhyme

to a little dusty room. This she surveys, noting with approval the dusty window that looks out on nothing more than an eyeless, dusty wall; and, pressing a half-crown into the damp, dusty hand, tells the boy it will serve.

She waits diligently till the descending footsteps have melted to silence, and the fat boy can be presumed to have resubmerged in the torpor from whence she stirred him; then she moves towards the room's one, dusty, mirror. She reaches with one large kid-gloved hand to release the buttons of the other.

Now what will we see? Now will be granted fragments of the veiled lady's secret? The hands from which the gloves are withdrawn are brown – not the brown of the Brahmin or the African, but the brown of the European unsheltered from a foreign sun. Where have her hands been to have returned so stained? The curious ring she wears (not on the wedding finger) may tell us. Yes, it is North African work; the beaten silver whorls murmur softly to us the word : "Morocco".

Enough of the hands. They have performed their small betrayal and told us all they know. But still they can help us, as they move up to detach the veil and reveal a new informer, the lady's face. It is a sad face they unshroud, a face of suffering; it is a face, too, that in some way not to be defined, is familiar to us. It is a face that has known pain – not only the distant pains of adversity, but also the more recent pains of... what? Is it illness? Not quite. No, it is a face that has recently suffered the pains of the surgeon's knife.

But can we know why the scalpel, saw and knife were needed? Surely, we insist, it must have been an illness that laid the veiled lady low. Her face denies that; it is too robust, too strong. Her face seems to whisper that, whatever operation she has so recently suffered, it was undertaken voluntarily.

The strangeness of these messages confuses us. Can we ever solve this conundrum, sort out the bizarre

fragments from wastepaper baskets

contradictions of the information the hands and face have confessed to us? Without more help, I fear not.

But, even as we think this, arrives that help, like a refreshing breeze lifting the dust of this hot, dusty day. The lady speaks, at once untangling the muddled skeins of our conjecture. She looks at her heavy-browed eyes in the dusty mirror, and, with a smile like an evening shadow stealing across her face, murmurs, "Welcome back to England, Edwina Drood."

WHYDIDNTTHEYDUNNIT?

As a lover of mystery fiction, I am not only delighted by the number of authors who have written in the genre, but also saddened by the number who haven't. Many of our literary greats were so busy doing what brought them fame and fortune that they never got round to writing whodunnits.

This is a situation that I decided should be remedied. If the authors never found time to do it themselves, then someone else would have to do it for them. It didn't take long for me to decide that that someone should be me.

At one stage I contemplated a whole book of such works. I even had a title for it – *Whydidnttheydunnit?*

Maybe one day I will write that book. In the meantime, here are a few tasters – mystery fiction by writers who never quite got round to writing it themselves.

A crime in rhyme

THE MYSTERIES OF T.S. ELIOT

Writing in the mystery genre is not easy, as many eminent authors have found to their cost. T.S.Eliot may have achieved a good title in "Murder in the Cathedral", but, as a whodunnit, the work leaves a lot to be desired. The same can be said of his earlier attempt - also with a good mystery title - "Murder in the Cathedral Close", of which a fragment has recently been discovered in the vault of the bank where Eliot used to work. By 1922, from when this piece dates, Agatha Christie had produced a mystery as sophisticated as "The Mysterious Affair at Styles." The inadequacy of Eliot's attempt in the genre can be demonstrated by this extract from The First Detective's summing-up in the book's final chapter.

Whydidn'ttheydunnit?

First Detective
So here in the library you stand,
Like corpses in their trays around a mortuary,
Dry with dust,
Apprehensive at the prospect of futurity.

TIME, GENTLEMEN, PLEASE.

There will be time for murder and arrest.
They've called for Sweeney and he's on patrol,
While here a culprit buttons up his vest,
And spoons out sugar from the sugar bowl.

TIME, GENTLEMEN, PLEASE.

Crime present and crime past
May help to unravel crime future
Though crime future may not always be crime solved.

Martini e Rossi Asti Spumante

Now for the victim, a dead weight in a dry time,
A ring of paper flowers around his bone,
His life's long rest has become silence,
Like a needle picked up suddenly from a gramophone.

TIME, GENTLEMEN, PLEASE.

Mr. Demosthenes, the sausage merchant,
Unloved, with vowels from the gutter,
Met his end at the end of a kitchen knife,
And one of you's responsible.

One of you saw something. What,
You saw nothing? Now you see nothing? Will you tell me

A crime in rhyme

Nothing?

> *Et maintenant les flics*
> *Se demandent qu'est-ce qu'il y a,*
> *Ses fusils fantastiques*
> *En portant dans les bras.*

Suspects now. There will be a time for suspects.
Burbank with a hunting knife.
Bleistein with a sword
Or Prufrock with an instrument,
Blunt as *smorgabord*?

The corpse you buried last month in your garden,
Has it begun to smell? Will it reappear?
Or has the acid bath destroyed all trace?

Cuckoo, jug-jug, pu-we, to-witta-woo!

Rogan ghosh.

I have called in the forensic boyos and
They have measured out the blood on coffee spoons

But

O O O O that Hohomicidal Rag -

Mercifully, the above is all that remains of "Murder in the Cathedral Close." It is believed to be Eliot's last attempt in the genre, and helped him to recognise his inadequacies as a mystery writer. And it was of course around the same time Agatha Christie gave up her attempts to write abstruse poetry. Scholars are still searching for the lost manuscript of her final effort, "Who Killed J. Alfred Prufrock?"

A crime in rhyme

One of my favourite writers in English is Thomas Hood. He lived from 1799 to 1845, and I was honoured to take part in a celebratory reading of his work on 23 May 1999, his two hundredth birthday.

I first came across Hood's work when I was writing the second of my Charles Paris novels, *So Much Blood*, in which I was planning to take my detective hero to the Fringe of the Edinburgh Festival. I needed a literary figure about whom Charles could do a one-man lunchtime show, and a friend, Chris Miller, suggested Thomas Hood. I read, loved what I read, and a lifetime passion was started.

Now sadly neglected, Hood was hugely popular well into the twentieth century. His work encompassed the comic and the tragic. Even people who might claim never to have heard of him would probably recognise some of his best-known poems, like *No-vember* or the one that begins, "I remember, I remember the house where I was born." He also wrote famous poems of social protest – *The Song of the Shirt* and *The Bridge of Sighs*.

But he is probably best known for his comic verse. Thomas Hood was one of the most sublime punsters in the English language. The Victorians loved puns and, even nowadays when they're slightly out of fashion, many people remain closet pun-lovers. I'm one of them, and I particularly enjoy Thomas Hood's "Pathetic Ballads", mock-tragic recitations, whose verse usually end with a particularly excruciating pun. For example :

> Ben Battle was a soldier bold,
> And used to war's alarms;
> But a cannon ball took off his legs,
> So he laid down his arms!"

More famous perhaps is :

> "His death, which happened in his berth,
> At forty-odd befell:
> They went and told the sexton, and
> The sexton toll'd the bell."

For a mystery-lover and pun-lover like me, the temptation was too great. So far as I knew, nobody had ever written a whodunnit in "Pathetic Ballad" form. Something had to be done about it.

THE DEATH OF DOREEN
Or, Dirty Doings in the Soup Kitchen
A Pathetic Ballad

The Great Detective on a case
Hissed in his Sergeant's ear,
On sniffing smells of *bouillabaisse*,
"There's something fishy here.

"The source of this smell of sauce, I surmise,
Is in this little cottage."
And inside was a sight for private eyes –
An awful mess of pottage.

The fish soup bubbled – cheery sound! –
But a supine girl lay dead
In a pool of fluid on the ground,
With a saucepan on her head.

"Taste it!" The Sergeant bravely tried,
And a furrow creased his brow.
"It's bean soup, sir." The Detective cried,
"I know. What is it now?"

"A lentil soup pan jammed down tight…
You realise what this means?"
"If we can free her head, it might
Just make her spill the beans."

Whydidn'ttheydunnit?

With care they prised her fair head out,
Felt her wrist, and let it fall.
Though peas and beans lay all about,
There was no pulse at all.

The Sergeant looked. "O Soup Doreen!"
He cried. "My lover dear!
We swore upon the soup tureen
We'd love through thick and clear!

"My broth of a girl! My best of colleens!
We were to be married – but how?
She's had her chips, she's had her beans,
And she's a has-been now!"

The Detective's brain was tickin'.
"Come on, you'd better tell.
Was the soup a cream of chicken
Or perhaps… *crime passionel?*

"See – she's been hit with a ladle.
That's how she lost her life."
"But I loved her from the cradle –
That was no ladle, that was my wife!"

But, weeping, the Sergeant wondered.
One thing did him bewilder;
And, after a flash, he thundered :
"How d'you know a ladle killed 'er?"

To err is human, you've heard,
And to forgive divine.
The Detective ummed and erred,
But his guilt through the dross did shine.

A crime in rhyme

The Sergeant came to the boil,
Found a ladle with a stain,
All wrapped in kitchen foil,
And his boss cried, "Foiled again!"

The Sergeant said, "Here's evidence
No lawyer can annul.
This ladle made the heavy dents
We see in the poor tart's skull."

The Detective turned bright red
And, while he stood there flustered, he
Heard his rights, and the Sergeant said,
"You are now a coward in custody."

The Sergeant felt glee and dejection.
His triumph brought pain to his heart,
Though his consummate art of detection
Had revenged his *consommé* tart.

The Detective was apprehended,
Doreen avenged, poor cow;
And, thanks to the soup, her intended
'S a Superintendent now.

The authors I most admire – Jane Austen, Evelyn Waugh and Raymond Chandler – all demonstrate the same skills – economy, and the ability to use humour to do more than just be funny.

Isn't it a terrible pity that Jane Austen never wrote a crime novel?

Or maybe she did just start one…?

HOME AND HOMICIDE
Chapter One

Lydia Bascombe, beautiful, intelligent, and wealthy, with evidently doting parents and a generous financial sufficiency, seemed to unite every blessing of ease and prosperity; and, at twenty-one years of age, might have expected throughout her life the continuation of such felicity; but for the fact that she was dead.

She lay, with as much decorum as her unfortunate condition allowed, on the floor of the withdrawing room at Upperfield Hall, beneath the pianoforte, upon which, in happier times, she had tested to the limits the appreciation of all visitors to that handsome and commodious abode. Tightly – in the circumstances regrettably tightly – about her slender neck was knotted a gentleman's neckerchief.

The family of Bascombe had not long been settled in Hampshire. Though their money had yet to attain the antiquity which might admit them to the best houses of the county, they contrived nonetheless to pass themselves off to the incurious as established members of the lesser gentry.

Mr. Bascombe was a native of London; in conversation, however, he avoided specificity as to which quarter of that fine and populous metropolis. Though, in middle age, naturally matured beyond such misfortune, Mr. Bascombe's general gruffness in society, and occasional lapses into a manner that fell but little short of coarseness, intimated that he might, at an earlier period of his life, have *worked* for his living; a supposition reinforced by the intermittent outbursts of a temper too robust for the conformities of polite usage.

Whether his anger might, under appropriate provocation, have been translated into violence; and whether that violence might have been directed against one of his own blood, towards whom the precepts of religion might be deemed to invite a particularity of cherishment; are both questions worthy of intense consideration by those curious to discover the cause of his daughter's sudden demise.

If Mr. Bascombe's defects of character might qualify him for the description of a rough diamond, he was possessed of a wife, whose endeavour it was to provide a glittering setting for such a flawed brilliant. However, deficient in the taste and discrimination which can only come with breeding, Mrs. Bascombe offered a setting whose glitter was not commensurate with its true value; whose garishness, rather than detracting from them, drew attention to Mr. Bascombe's inadequacies; bringing no sparkle to the rough diamond, but rather raising the disturbing speculation that her husband might be a mere thing of paste.

It was the stedfast opinion of Mrs. Bascombe that every situation, however capable of discomfort, could be alleviated by a sufficiency of conversation; and she was generous enough in her nature to be believe that *she* should be the provider of the greatest part of that conversation. Every time, therefore, that her husband threatened to expose himself in society, she would commence to talk. This tendency towards conversational monopoly, together with the good lady's predilection for dress more suited to the theatre than the pump-room, made her the object of immoderate hilarity amongst the more socially secure of her Hampshire neighbours.

But whether vacuity, indelicacy, and lack of taste might mask more vicious shortcomings in Mrs. Bascombe was a question that could not readily be answered. Her manner towards Lydia had been frequently peremptory; but that a more extreme expression of impatience and pettishness

A crime in rhyme

might have led to the deliberate curtailment of her daughter's life was a conjecture that, at least in initial entertainment, must seem unlikely.

It is a truth universally acknowledged, that the murder of a young woman in a country house, must be in want of an investigator.

And, at the moment of Lydia Bascombe's untimely encounter with her Maker, by good fortune, such a personage was of the company at Upperfield Hall. He was a gentleman of independent means, whose acuity of intellect and facility of address was marred only by a haughtiness, which seemed to imply that those around him not only suffered from a quality of understanding far beneath his own, but indeed belonged to an inferior species. The name of this paragon was…

And there, sadly, the frail manuscript ends. Miss Austen, no doubt called away from her writing desk to entertain visitors, found possibly, on her return to the work in progress, that she longer cared a fig who killed Lydia Bascombe.

A crime in rhyme

A few years ago, Swansea was designated "The City of Literature", and that small Welsh metropolis became the host for an entire year of writer-related events. One week was devoted to crime fiction, and I was delighted to be invited, along with fellow theatrical mystery writer Simon Shaw, to contribute a cabaret routine we performed from time to time, called *Acting in a Suspicious Manner*.

When I heard that the venue for our presentation was to be the Dylan Thomas Theatre, I'm afraid I decided that a new piece of material would have to be written specially for the occasion...

UNDER MURDER WOOD

First Voice
To begin with the murder. It is dawn, streaky day-burst bubbling and boring through the bog of the night, lifting the cloud-cloak, curtain-back and good-morning dawning rise of the slip-shod, slipper-footed, dressing-gown-garbed, early-morning-tea, slap-of-the-papers-on-the-"Welcome"-mat, light-up-a-cigarette dawn, in the little town of Lludicrys. All over the town, alarm clocks are crowing, toothpaste-tubes squeezing, kippers grilling, cereals soggying, and old men spitting at Jones and Evans, Vitreous Enamel, Merthyr Tydfil. Every opening eye and waking heart stirs and stretches and creaks and uncrumples to the beauty of another do-it-or-drop-it day. Every eye but one.

Second Voice
Dai the Death alone ignores the morning.

First Voice
Because he is dead.

Second Voice
Dead down the mine. Down in the doom gloom brown bowel, deep beneath the stomach of the turgid stirring, slow churning earth.

First Voice
But what is he thinking, Dai the Death?

A crime in rhyme

Second Voice
He is thinking of nothing, because he is dead. The dead are tight as misers' purse-strings with the bunched-up bounty of their bibled thoughts.

First Voice
But if he were alive, what would he be thinking, Dai the Death? Only you can hear his thoughts.

Second Voice
He would think what he thought day-long down the mine, as time ticked by, unmarked by the daylight and night, but by the flickering of his Davy Lamp quick across the slack, as his pick knocked quick at rock blocks of coal, and showers of little bits trickled to his feet. If he were alive. But he is dead. So what unthinkable, unthankful thoughts is he thinking now in the coal-hole gloom of his dusty dreams?

First Voice
Never such dreams as any that come in the mournful morning of murder. Never such ends as any that end in the coal-axe poleaxed through the walnut shell of his cranium into the unripe soft fruit of his wicked-dreaming brain. Never such sudden stopping of his thoughts, his naughty, palm-sweating, hand-groping, hem-lifting, beard-tickling, dirty postcard pictures of...

Dai The Death
Blodwyn Jenkins. Oh, Blodwyn, Blodwyn, Blodwyn J...

First Voice
At the other side of the town, in the tight, cotton-ticked, up-to-the-chin-tucked, false-teeth-clicked-in-the-glass, unalarm-clocked silence, Detective Inspector Taff the Truncheon, is woken from a dream of...

Taff The Truncheon
Petty thieving, minor traffic infringements, fines for overdue library books, telling the time to tourists, commendations for bravery and... an engraved barometer...

First Voice
...by the thrilling, sleep-killing trill of a truculent telephone - and the news that...

Second Voice
Dai the Death has been...

First Voice
...murdered!

Taff The Truncheon
"Murdered" is it you say? "Murdered"? But that's a terrible word to be heard by a man still in his flanelette nightgown. Ring me again, when I have my uniform on.

First Voice
And as he bustles into blue, buckling his belly taut with the black leather, heaving on hearse-black boots, hefting his helmet high on the cramped dome of his cranium...

Second Voice
...he hears wafting, through the window, the words of a morning poem...

Meredith The Murder
There may be greater towns than ours,
With fiercer and more famous sons,
And higher rates of homicide,
More people armed with knives and guns;

A crime in rhyme

And yet, for me, this blessed place
As scene of crime can have no peer.
Let others inner cities haunt -
I'll still brain all my victims here.

Second Voice
And –

Taff The Truncheon
"Oh..."

First Voice
Cries Taff the Truncheon...

Taff The Truncheon
"I think that could be a clue."

First Voice
And he goes out through the trim letterbox-rattling, catch-clicking, knocker-knocking frame of his front door...

Second Voice
To visit Meredith the Murder...

First Voice
And says...

Taff The Truncheon
"I keep thinking there must be a clue in your name, Meredith, though I'm damned if I know what it is."

First Voice
But he still arrests him.

Second Voice
Again. As he has done every bloody-bodied day of the corpse-covered, shroud-shocking year.

First Voice
And the afternoon dies and the thin light fades. And Taff the Truncheon, roundly righteous, crammed with complacency, rumbling with rectitude, fulfilled in flanelette, snores down the slope of his sleep, knowing that tomorrow he could have a...

Taff The Truncheon *(Sleepily)*
"'Nother cadaver..."

First Voice
And the sky once again velvets to darkness over the silver-tapped blood-bath of the little night-winking town.